Casa Blanca Lily

For my mother, the true embodiment of strength

The Casa Blanca Lily is a beautiful fragrant flower that blooms at night. In the darkness when other flowers go into a sleeplike state of nyctinasty, this lily reveals its large gleaming white petals that symbolize virtue and purity.

One of the most regal flowers widely revered for its allure blooms in the absence of light.

Casa Blanca Lily started as a kind of diary, hence the untraditional writing style. It was a means to an end, my attempt to unravel myself and reel in my fervent emotions. Then I decided it to share it with anyone willing to listen, to feel heartbreak, failures, and insecurities amplified by honesty.

I can only hope that my journey to sanity echoes through these pages, as the girl who started writing this book turned into a different woman by the final keystroke. I blossomed during the darkest phase of my life when I was living tepidly, afraid of who I was and what I felt.

So this is it, my beautiful ugly journey, the one I should be ashamed to share but knowing I am no longer this person has emboldened me in ways I could've never imagined.

I hope you enjoy.

The Unloved

Love

My demon crawled up my faith-laden precipice
to tell me that I was unloved and I listened. My
obedience to all things ugly and hurtful forced me
to believe it.

I was unloved.

Immeasurable desperation soon forced me to seek
love from the pits of hell, hoping that my demon
had friends who could love me again.

The Toxicity of Brokenness

"What's the saddest thing you've ever seen?"

"People who are unknowingly enslaved by their affliction," she said as she hands me a needle from her small leather pouch filled with heroin paraphernalia. Scornfully, I hold the syringe as I watch her bring a lighter to the bottom of the metal spoon heating the black tar heroin above it.

She gestures for me to hand the hypodermic needle back to her, but I hesitate, bracing myself for her ire.

"What the fuck give it to me now or I will gouge your eyes out."

"Please don't, you're killing yourself. Don't do this anymore."

"I'm already dead," she says with such conviction I start to wonder if she knows she's alive.

She grabs the syringe from my hand, wets a cotton ball with some alcohol, and rubs it over the bend of her arm. She fills the syringe with the substance in the spoon then places it flat against her skin as she slowly pushes down on the plunger. Her eyes widen as she starts gaping at the blank wall in front of us.

13

"See kid, I told you –already dead," she grins soullessly as her eyes roll back and she slumps against my shoulder.

It was the first time I ever saw someone so broken chase a release just as toxic as what had broken them. It made me think about how far we'd go to erase old scars even if it meant creating new ones.

Forever Until Today

Disillusionment ran through me like a fire in a torrid forest, turning expectations into useless soot as the truth rose to meet my eyes.

Lucid dreams of us grey and hale retelling our tale to jaded ears was replaced by the empty hangers in *our* closet and pristine sheets on the other side of *our* bed.

How To Forget

I deleted his number for the last time even though I had it memorized. So I set a new goal for myself, to use liquor to erase the digits from my mind. All that did was put me into a deep slumber where I had no thoughts and no concept of time.

So when I awoke the pain felt fresh, renewed and energized, hell-bent on ruining my life.

We Praise Angels But We Love Demons

I saw you once and scribbled your name into the
margins of my life. Wishing I could write it like a
title, bold and deep across my heart. You were a
dream, the hopelessly unattainable. An
unquenchable thirst that emptied me of the desire
to be with anyone else.

You heard my desperation and answered my
dream with a nightmare. You rummaged through
my soul, harassed my self-esteem and I forgave in
the name of love.

It ended abruptly.

I don't remember how or why just that the poison
that trickled from the tip of your tongue left me
curled on the floor in my own tears for many long
months. It was there in the sobriety of my
heartbreak that I realized sometimes we invite
demons into our lives and try as we might, we
can't love them back into angels.

They are dangerously beautiful, shaded with
mischief and chaos, cursed by the string of broken
hearts they've left behind.

Explain

I knew he was cheating, cheaters never change,
but I also knew I craved him –he was cocaine.

Ticking Clock

I was a spectator in their love story, a blurred face in a sea of wishful onlookers. She was a friend, a girl who rushed through life with a carelessness that almost made her seem unhinged. So when he placed his commitment on her finger, her world slowed.

"How does it feel to know that you have someone for the rest of your life?" I asked.

"I can't explain it. I never understood how people could cry when they were happy until now," she said as the tears escaped her eyes.

I hid my envy behind a gulp of my wine and excused myself to somewhere private where I could cry, but my tears were the sorrowful kind. I stood on the cold balcony alone and jealous until I heard someone clearing their throat behind me. Announcing his intrusion was her fiancé. He looked just as unhappy as I did. So we fell into an easy conversation, using each other as emotional crutches.

Finally, I asked, "What's it like to know you'll have her for the rest of your life?"

"Scary," he replied, "but I need to be married before I turn thirty-five."

My envy receded. I looked at him and I saw the honesty, it was not love that brought them together, it was the fear of being alone. I wanted to tell her what he said, but when I saw her again, the truth started to dance in my mouth. I became tongue-tied.

It made me realize, I never want to be with someone who settles for me because they are running out of time.

Your Seed

Planting a seed in a dying garden will never
revive it. Limiting that flower to a panoramic
view of the casualties of your heartbreak is a
tasteless, selfish thing to do.

I know this, for I once thought salvation could
grow in me, belie reality and keep me attached to
you.

Dilemma

I can't do it. I simply cannot. My family will hate me for bringing this disgrace to their doorsteps and God will punish me for being unwed. He'll also punish me for murder. For spitting in his face the ability to bear fruit in his garden.

I must not. I must not carry into this world the flesh of a human I cannot love. I don't even know how it happened, it was all a mistake. I am an adult it is my decision to make. Am I *unmotherly* because I do not want this?

It's not illegal to rid myself of the unwanted but I am stuck questioning my morality. I know what I want to do, but I am afraid of the judgment, the slant eyes, the lewd remarks, the knowing of not knowing what it could've become. I don't want to do this again, I know I cannot do it again. Can God forgive me, if sin is sin, all equally rebuked in heaven?

What choice have you given me? Both alike in their dishonor, the secrecy of a woman's most intimate moment put on trial to my horror.

A moment of indiscretion extended into a lifetime. Imprisoned by archaic moral codes, I am scared –please don't let me choose between death and dishonor.

Repeat After Me

He looked at me and I knew he saw the clenched jaw, and tear-brimmed eyes. I wanted to yell at him for hurting me, to butcher him the way he had butchered me, but I couldn't.

I didn't want to lose him. My truth would have pushed him over the edge. So I steadied my breath and calmed myself. I was already convinced. Convinced that if I lost him I'd never find love again.

It's the beautiful witchcraft he cast on me, the whispers I could hear. He said it so often my subconscious started to tell me the same thing. That one lie he shared as a truth. His favorite sentence to stab me with after every argument:

"You'll never find anyone who loves you like this again."

Affirmation

"Do you want to ruffle the sheets with me?"

"Yes."

"Do you want to dance drunkenly between the palm trees with me?"

"Yes."

"Do you want to blow through forever carelessly with me?"

"Yes."

"Do you want to smoke cigarettes outside of church with me?"

"Yes."

"Do you want to deface the sidewalk with vomit and profanity with me?"

"Yes."

"When we've done it all, seen everything, hurt each other, slit our throats with bitter jealousy will you leave me?"

"Yes."

Time Stamps

3:00 a.m. I am sprinting through the deserted L.A. streets. The cool air, thick and heavy, like my emotions. I am running to nowhere but I am running from him.

2:00 a.m. I still couldn't fall asleep, so I texted him, *I miss you, baby, call me.* He didn't respond so I took it upon myself to drive over there, surprise him but he surprised me.

2:20 a.m. I am outside, calling him, the phone keeps ringing, but he doesn't answer me. Then I see his neighbor Vinny stumbling in from a long night of sleeping, drinking, maybe even fucking.

"Hey Vin, can you let me in?"

"No problem, I'm sure he just fell asleep."

2.30 a.m. I am at his door, I think to knock but I hear muffled moaning. *What is he watching?*

2:32 a.m. I open his door, I'm greeted by filigree white panties tossed on the floor, a linen shirt strewed over his couch, six-inch stilettos on the coffee table and still no him just low erotic moaning. His apartment smells like bourbon or whiskey, the one that I hate but she loves. There's Lolita open on the counter and a scarf by the bedroom door.

2:36 a.m. I walk into his bedroom. She's on her knees bent over, craving him, blindfolded but facing me. He's focused on her ass, giving her the extension of his virility. I am surprisingly not surprised by what I am seeing. He finally looks up and stops moving when he realizes he's not dreaming –I am not an intrusion of his wild fantasies, I am here. She asks him, *baby, what's wrong?* And he says nothing, prompting her to pull her blindfold off and see the haunted bitch – me.

2:40 a.m. We're all transfixed by the situation, but she being his longest memory is the first to speak.

"Is this her –your little friend?" Her condescending tone is all the answer I need, clearly, he spoke so little of me that she thinks I am nothing, I am nobody. He pulls out of her, slowly sits on the bed, and buries his face in his hands. She's happy and carefree, so she kisses him on the cheek.

"I'll give you a second to tell her," she smiles a dirty grin then brushes by me. She's so unbothered that she starts to play music in the living room and I can hear her dancing around, naked, waiting for me to leave.

2:50 a.m. I'm still stuck in his doorway. He lifts his head and I see his explanation. I was just a pastime until she was free, single, ready for him again. I should've known he's like a swan with the ability to only fall in love once –she was his once. He rises to his feet, takes a deep breath but before the hurtful truth finds its place in the static air between us. I run away.

4:00 a.m. I am still running.

Ego

My fingers have grazed the finest most delicate
samples of Chantilly lace and even that is sturdier
than a man's ego.

The composition of a man is half cement, half
gravel. A man is an indefatigable being with
unyielding confidence and faith in his
capabilities.

A man is a provider, the planter, and the gleaner
of his fruitful harvest. Where the firm lines of his
body illustrate strength, a woman's curves leave
her vulnerable, begging for a man's help.

Ego Restored

He used the shards of my broken heart to open
me up. He was more fascinated with the anatomy
of my brokenness than anything else.

He salivated hearing my shallow breaths
disappear into pain-stricken moans.

The delectable and exquisite torture of seeing me,
the one who he once yearned for, suddenly
desperate for him, desperate for his love. It must
have restored his ego. The same ego that I bruised
by refusing him once.

Polarity

One rainy night parked under the flickering streetlight in front of my apartment. I asked him *the question*.

"Where do you see this going?"

His eyes darted from mine to the steering wheel. I could see him constructing the nicest way to hurt my feelings.

"I don't know, let's not complicate things with titles," he replied.

"Okay."

I tried my best to downplay the sinking feeling in my stomach, the hot tears burning the back of my eyes and the deflation of my lungs. I gave him a toothless smile and a tight nod.

He continued to talk about how his day went, while I stared outside onto the glistening pavement.

Punishment

The pseudo-oblivious lover, who claims they can't tell when they're hurting you is actually a sadist.

Nothing makes their orgasm more intense, than bludgeoning your feelings and watching you martyr yourself over arguments and events that they pretend they didn't know would hurt you like this.

Discount Virgin

"Shouldn't we wait?"

"For what?"

"I don't know, for it to feel right."

"Forget this, trying to sleep with you was a waste of my time."

So I told him to do it, hoping he wouldn't be angry anymore. I bargained with my virginity for a boy I didn't even love.

Fake It

Sex is for men, it must be.

I've had them fill me with themselves, empty
their souls into my body while I just stare at the
ceiling, lachrymose and tired, waiting for it to
end. I'm a vessel for their orgasms, my pleasure
too high a price to pay.

Not enjoying sex is my shame for if I
communicate this to them then I am the problem.
I am the one who is broken. So when you ask me
if I like sex, I'm afraid I don't know what you
mean.

Women are things to *fuck* not people to please.

Thief

At first, he was gentle, flowers on a Monday and dinners at sunset. He saw my soul when others only saw my skin, this was love, –I was in love. Anything he wanted I felt like I would give to him. Men have a weird way of making simple women like me feel complete.

The days turned to weeks, when one night parked outside of my parents' house, he finally asked. He wanted that piece of me that I wasn't ready to give, but his eyes peeled away the layers of my doubt as his hands twirled the ends of my hair.

He turned on the radio and we listened to Etta James' *At Last* pour through the stereo. The infectious beat coupled with Etta's soothing voice diffused the sting of what he wanted from me. He reached around to the back seat and pulled forward a brown paper bag. Peeking from the top was a gold wrapped cork. He smiled as he fidgeted with the cork until we jolted in surprise from the loud pop.

"Here," he said with warm eager eyes.

Hesitant but curious, I tilted the bubbly liquid to my head and giggled with enjoyment as the crisp carbonated fluid filled my stomach. Sip after sip we laughed harder and longer at his subpar jokes until finally everything went dark.

The next morning a pounding headache greeted my consciousness with a hard shake. I tried to stretch but an unfamiliar soreness quickly forced me to keep still. Before I could gather my scattered thoughts, out he came with his boxers hanging dangerously low. His hair tousled with dampened strands sweeping across his forehead. His calmness contrasted my pulsating heart and coiled fear.

He gave me a wink and started getting ready, the silence crackling with the impending sting of rejection I was sure would come. He pulled his shirt over his head and when he was fully clothed, he walked over to me and sat on the edge of my bed. With his back turned to me he slipped on his shoes.

"I'll call you okay?" he muttered as he tied his laces.

I watched helplessly as he walked away with what he had stolen.

In The Eyes Of God

Yesterday in church, the pastor spoke about
obedience. Listening to your spouse and parents
was the best way to honor God he said. I scoffed
at the sermon as I tried to remember a time when
my parents listened to me or the last time my
father valued my mother's opinion.

Yet, there we were applauding, saying *Amen,*
speaking in tongues, pretending we practiced
what he preached.

Play

If only they told me sooner the lies we live inevitably become our truth. Bare-chested and fat rosy cheeks, with sagging diapers sloshing around, we ran wildly. Frolicking pigtails and starry eyes, presented as little girls. Damsel in distress waiting for a prince to slay our invisible dragons, taught to not only depend on, but also expect salvation.

We put Band-Aids on plastic limbs and hushed our *Seussian* kids. We played in dusty blushes and stole our mother's crimson lips. We blistered our toes on wooden floors and hid the stains deep within our pointe shoes. We spent Sunday afternoons baking cookies in plastic ovens and served them to our imaginary friends.

Every now and then, we heard the boys outside. So we peaked through windowpanes watching them play in dirt as we should expect. The first time we noticed we were born into a world where we would be confined to its systematic problems.

We played the role: curtsied, frolicked, and dumbed ourselves down to look pretty. We did it so effortlessly it became the lucid lie we lived.

So now I hope you understand why I have no voice, why I can't speak. I was taught how to live prettily and silently.

Enough

I was transparent, he saw right through me and even though I could wet his tongue, he was still thirsty.

I, the stanza of a forgotten poem, she, the novel – he was eager to turn her pages.

Like honey, her name coated his tongue, while mine, like bile, bitter and sour was the venom he had to spit out.

Uncommon Things

I wasn't her.

I didn't speak his language, I knew nothing about everything he loved. Forever misplaced in his conversations. She, on the other hand, was fluent in him and even though they were over, I saw how much he missed it.

I was far too limpid for his tastes, nothing to unveil, everything clear and on display. She, mysterious and dark, the allure of a woman like her too large a space for me to fill.

I know deep down he doesn't love me. I am a common thing that he will eventually get bored with.

Marred by The Married Lover

Our lips finally separated after what felt like an eternity of kissing. Confined to the back of his car, the streetlights are barely bright enough for me to see his face. I can sense that he is contrite; his amorous touch lacks the usual burn of desire.

"What's wrong?" I lean back into the seat giving him space to gather any scattered thoughts.

"I can't leave her."

Suddenly, the back of his car is too large. I shrink to nothing as his words jitter through my brain. My smallness making me hyper-aware of my heated blush. In a nervous gesture, I start to pick invisible lint off the edge of my seat. My throat arid and tight from the sudden discomfort of his confession.

"But you said," I don't need to finish my sentence because he knows. He knows that three months ago when he came up to me in the coffee shop that I was skeptical of the tan line around his ring finger. I was never that girl, but two teas later he explained that he was separated from his wife and that their divorce was almost finalized.

"My wife and I are going to try again, this was fun though."

The rehearsed opening line of his breakup speech is hard to listen to, especially since this is the first time he mentions her as his *wife* and not his *ex*. My stomach churns so I open the back door and exit his car. I make it about ten steps when I turn my head to the hedges and vomit. The liquefied dejection pours out of me like a raging stream. As my retching dies down, I start to worry. I worry that the man I love is about to leave me for the woman he belongs to. His gilded life and wife, outweighing the shallow connection we have –I mean had. His engine disrupts the throbbing in my ears, I want to look back but I am too weak. His headlights flash on and cast a shadow over my feeble body. His wheels splash into the puddles as he drives away, leaving me and my puke covered shoes to walk home.

When I start to regain some strength, I pull my phone from my back pocket and call a cab. I know I smell like death but I'm ten miles away from home and it's 11:00 p.m.; when the cab arrives the driver eyes me warily. I quickly explain that when he drops me home I will go upstairs, get my purse and not only compensate him but give him a hefty tip. He lets me into the car and I see his nose twitch from the stench of my vomit sodden shoes. All I can think about while the driver silently navigates his way through the dark streets is him. My lover who left me marred and alone. I start to wonder where I went wrong, the self-deprecation tearing through the fragments of my broken heart. *Maybe if I listened more –maybe*

*the sex wasn't good enough —maybe it was the way I
laughed —maybe it was my eyes —maybe I just didn't
know where I went wrong.*

 I need an explanation. I tap the cab driver on his
shoulder and tell him my new plan, he looks
displeased and impatient, but I promise to double
the size of his tip if he does this for me. Without
answering, he slams his foot on the brakes and
makes a sharp right turn. I realize the direction he
is going and ease back into my seat.

There's a moment after one is rejected where
irrationality takes precedence. When we beat
ourselves into actions and thoughts that
subconsciously we know are wrong, but the pain
uproots all logic so we succumb to our own
foolishness. This was it for me.

When the cab pulls up outside of his castle, I see
that his car is parked neatly behind hers in the
driveway. Their unbreakable bond evident from
even outside, bile rises to the back of my throat as
I fight the urge to suppress my disgust. I slide out
of the cab after giving the driver a pointed look
and steady my gait towards his home.

His Parisian style iron wrought gate is open,
which doesn't surprise me, in a fancy
neighborhood like this the only crime that goes on
is having an unkempt lawn. The sleek driveway is
sandwiched between rhododendron bushes –its
beauty slowly pulls me deeper into my

commitment to see this through, step-by-step, I am spellbound by my heartbreak. This is a bad idea. I know it is. I should turn around, go home and cry into a pint of Ben & Jerry's, but I can't. I am already here and I am already broken.

I fold my arms around my chest, as the chilling reality of what I am about to do courses through my body. When I finally get to the house, there are no lights peeking through the window. I assume everyone is fast asleep. Once again, I know this is a bad idea, but how can I stop myself? After three hard loud knocks on his front door, I stand there shivering in fear and disbelief. While I wait for someone to answer the door my eyes drift around their front yard, my reconnaissance yields nothing of consequence.

Frankly, I don't know what I was expecting to see –maybe a wedding picture on their front lawn. I scoff at my ridiculousness. I hear shuffling inside and then the sound of the locks being undone. I squeeze my fists so tightly that my knuckles become white as the rest of my body carries the telltale flush of anger. I square my shoulders to give him the speech I've practiced in my mind on the way here. I lick my lips and straighten my skirt in a pathetic attempt to look unaffected by his rejection. I want him to remember me as the vixen, not the wench. The door creaks open and the light from the hallway inside shines onto my horrified face.

"How may I help you?"

She's wearing a silk light pink robe, her hair is tousled and falls over her shoulders. Her eyes are emerald green, even with thin veins of red strung around them from fatigue they are striking. Her perfectly sculpted lips and olive skin serve as an explanation. She's stunning, any man who leaves her would be mad, even I am surprised by her natural beauty. My faculties light up as the flush from my anger is replaced with embarrassment. I wasn't expecting her to come to the door. I open my mouth to speak but my breath catches and I start to suffocate. The reality of seeing his wife is stifling, it's too much. She stares at me doe-eyed awaiting my explanation, but it never comes.

"Honey what's going…" he says as he materializes behind his confused wife. She turns to look at him registering his recognition. I am now a passenger of my own plight.

"You know her? She's the woman you've been sleeping around with isn't she?"

He runs an agitated hand through his dark hair as he clenches his jaw; he peels his eyes away from his wounded wife as the anger burns through the tension between us.

"What the fuck do you want?" he spits. His words should have sent me running back to the cab, but I was rooted on his front steps.

Transfixed by the pain and realization of my situation.

"Don't speak to her like that!"

Both of our heads snap towards his wife as she folds her hands across her chest.

"Look at her! She had no idea that you were married –did you?" She turns her emerald green eyes to mine as I finally find my manners and a few words.

"He told me it was over –a divorce –he said you were getting a divorce –I mean –yeah that's what he said –I'm so sorry," I mutter.

She turns to him, crestfallen and addled. I know she is hurt and I feel horrendously guilty for bringing this to her front door. This feels personal like I've wronged a best friend or family member, she doesn't deserve this. I need to fix this.

"I'm lying," both of their heads turn to me, "I knew he was married. I'm sorry this is my fault, I was trying to make him leave you –he loves you so much –I just wanted to experience that."

The shame forces my eyes to one particular spot on the ground. I'm martyring myself right here to save their marriage, to save her. The fabulous house, the expensive car, the silk robe –I don't want to take that from her or force her to choose. I don't wait for her to say another word.

"I'm sorry, that's why I came here, he always refused me, saying how much he loved you –I needed to know what was so special about you, and now I do."

He's stunned, I'm sure the self-absorbed asshole that he is, he thinks I'm doing this for him but I'm doing it for her. I know what it's like to be alone, to be void, to see love and pray for it. I can't take that from her, not like this. I turn around, not giving them time to dissect my faux confession and run back to my cab. As my hand reaches for the handle of the door I feel a small tug on my shoulder. I turn around and she's standing behind me. Her eyes brimmed with tears and her lips quivering with words she wants to say.

 "Don't you ever come back. He loves me and you know that now, so if your little lie was to make him think you're good at keeping secrets so he can always rely on you to keep the affair private, you're wrong. He'll always choose me and you're nothing but a whore."

Her words sting and I'm disappointed that she thinks I lied to preserve a relationship with her husband. But for the first time in a couple of hours, I pity someone else.

"You're his wife, not a choice," I say with so much benevolence even I'm surprised.

 I leave her standing outside as my cab pulls away, standing there under the shadow of night and veil of shame. She looks like me. The *me* her husband left on the curb hours ago. She has that same gaunt stature that's caused by a man who values no one and a woman who's terrified to be alone.

Insecure Girls Always Stay

I waited for something he could never give. He pulled me through staining emotions and dirtied me with disappointment. But when he tried to leave I clung to the coattails of my toxic past because the future had not been written without him.

I knew that unrequited love was ruinous, flawlessly devastating, and incomparably afflictive, but what could I do?

Starting over with someone new felt wrong, the thought too hard to even accommodate.

It was a silly decision, but girls riddled with insecurities always find reasons to stay.

Grip

I hear them yelling through the drywall. It's the third time this week their arguments have spilled into my flat.

"Don't fucking touch me," she shouts.

"Just get out."

"No," she retorts, I imagine her arms are folded and her stance is stubborn.

"Fine, then I'll leave."

The door slams; I can hear him stomping down our dreary hall, eager to get away. My dog starts to bark from the commotion and restlessness, so I grab her leash and decide to take her for a walk. As soon as we get to the entryway of our apartment I see him. His brown curly hair flopping in the wind as he smokes, poisoning himself to burn out everything he's feeling.

His shoulders are rigid with tension and his cigarette free hand is balled into a tight fist. I yank my dog to the left, telepathically telling her to walk down the street, instead, she growls and lets out a deafening bark. He spins around and immediately the tension leaves his shoulders as he bends down to pet her.

"What is she?" he looks at me with a toothy smile that leaves me winded.

"A bitch," I reply shyly, but truthfully.

He starts to laugh, a hearty deep laugh that belies his taciturn mood. He straightens himself, drops the cigarette to the concrete pavement, and grinds his heel against it until it's out.

"*Bitch?*" he tests the word on his tongue with unresolved poignancy, "I know a couple of those."

"Well, she's the queen of the pack," I say as I point to my miserable dog who is itching to go for a walk.

"Can I join you?"

"What?"

"Can I walk with you? I need a distraction," he says as he nudges his head in the direction of our building.

"Sure," I shrug.

We walk almost six blocks in silence before we get back to our building. He stands outside, hesitant and wary. I don't know enough to make any helpful comments so I opt to extend the awkward silence.

"Sometimes it's good being around people who don't make you feel like the world's caving in," he says as he stares at my dog and I wonder if he's talking about her or me.

"It is."

Before I can delve deeper into the meaning of his statement, the front door swings open and his eyes start to glow. I turn around and she comes bouncing out. Her petite frame and chestnut hair crash into his arms.

"I'm so sorry Gabriel, I love you," she whispers as his hands slide over her shoulders to find their resting place in the small of her back.

"I love you too," he says as he tucks her head under his neck. He looks at me and gently shakes his head. I purse my lips together and head inside with my dog.

Two days later, I hear the telltale slamming of his door, this time his footsteps stop at my doorway. Eagerly, I press my body against the door and narrow my focus through the peephole.

He rocks from left to right before he raises his hand, my body tenses, he's about to knock when I hear her barreling towards him. Pulling him in like the ocean to its tide.

"I'm sorry Gabriel, I love you." It's the same story again. I watch as they reconcile for the millionth time.

Warning

Everything that's bad for us comes with a warning label. So where's yours? Where is the sign that says:

Warning! Try as you might this individual is toxic, produces unwavering heartbreak, and is destined to disappoint.

The Nature Of Things

The sky does not stop pouring because you've asked.

The seasons do not hastily retreat because you've asked.

The sea does not steady itself or shallow its depth because you've asked.

The sun does not burn gingerly because you've asked.

The moon does not shine lambently because you've asked.

So how is my heart to stop coveting your love because you've asked?

Meta-her

He couldn't love me as is, he had to love me as
her. He told me how to comb my hair, what
stockings to wear, the lexicon of love he preferred
–everything he told me to do was his way of
turning me into her.

All I wanted was him, I didn't need to exist. All
he wanted was her, he settled for this.

Insult

"You're such a romantic," he scoffed.

He thought I was nauseatingly saccharine. In his mind, I turned everything into meaningful intricate paths that I convinced myself led to some cathartic revelation about love. In one sentence, his message was clear I was emotionally inept, creating whimsical storylines and narratives out of thin air.

It was an insult, but then I looked at him. He was burdened with the bitter words and actions of people he'd trusted. He was a man unaware of how to deal with his feelings. A man shunned by his own heart, struggling to find his own remedy.

He was right about me and although I felt belittled, I realized the insult worked both ways, for if I was the naïve one who felt too much, he was the ailing soul who felt too little.

Happy Stories

He wanted to know me better so I read him my diary as if it were fiction. He loved the way my words crashed into his heart, scorched his brain, and simmered down into his soul. He said, my words meant more to him than my actions did because I wrote unhindered, exposed and truthfully. He said I was a wordsmith, attaching incomparable descriptions to moments he reduced to colloquialisms.

He said my writing was the single most fascinating part of my existence. It was a talent. He was convinced that the way my words filled blank pages was truly sorcery, magical in its execution leaving him absolutely spellbound. There was only one problem with my words.

My words were not flowery or light. He said that was the flaw with everything I've ever written and he would eventually tire of it. *No one likes to constantly read sad stories* was the argument he made when he tried to convince me to write happier things. But these weren't just stories, they were a part of my life.

I knew he could never love me then, but I had to ask him.

 "Are you happy? Do you actually know what it is like to be so free, so honest, and so content, that you can veraciously proclaim happiness? Man is so hungry for happiness that we've lessened its value. We now associate the theory of happiness to perishable things like money, sex, and power. We've printed the value of happiness on paper, fucked our way to orgasms that exhaust us and corrupted our morals all in pursuit of some elusive happiness."

"But you can't always be that sad?"

"And what if I am?"

He said nothing more about my words, and I don't know if it was because he stopped loving them or saw the darkness and stopped loving me. But I never stopped writing my sad stories, even if he no longer wanted to read.

I was okay with idea that my writing would probably be only for my eyes to see.

Bone Dry

"Bleed for me," he says as he pulls the blade across my virgin wrists. At first, it hurts then I slowly feel the release. The pressure escaping invites buoyancy. I step outside of myself to capture the scene and what I see scares me. My body limp, wrists leaking, eyes gaunt, and him grinning cheek to cheek.

I want to shake myself out of this trance and rebuke this vampire from my life. But his almond-shaped green eyes and sharp teeth are far too exquisite. His pale skin and soft hands turn me on.

 It's too late, I'm his prisoner now.

Distance

"You want to leave me, don't you?" I asked as I unpacked our groceries.

I could feel his eyes boring into my back but I was too scared to face him and the truth.

"No –I love you," he said and walked off.

But we both knew.

We knew that as much as we loved each other we weren't meant to be together. We'd grown so much as individuals that we were strangers sleeping in the same bed, lovers who only knew how to have sex.

Comfortable

We lay next to each other, fingers intertwined. It felt as if I had finally done something right. My dolefulness replaced with unending optimism and hope. Hope, that I'd never feel frayed or alone again. My perpetual singularity finally ending.

But comfort never lasts, it's a fleeting moment we extend for as long as we can. Knowing that the things we love the most have the shortest lifespans.

Don't Call

*If you miss someone call them and if you love someone
tell them.*

I pick up the phone and dial your number; my
finger perched on the call sign. My heart flutters
when I think of your silky voice on the other line
and how I'd breathe heavily into the microphone,
already winded. We would laugh and talk and I
would find solace in us.

But it doesn't work like that, does it?

One digit at a time I delete your haunted number
from the screen. I stare at the vacant space that
your caller ID once occupied and think, *if you miss
someone call them and if you love someone tell them
and he hasn't called to say anything*.

I Don't Exist

He deleted me.

With one click, two years of a relationship disappeared from the world. I refreshed his page repeatedly, hoping the remnants of what we were would resurface, but it never did.

I was gone –we didn't exist.

That's what the end looks like; erasure, deleting me virtually was his declaration of singleness.

Tell Me We're Not Over

Gingerly, I placed my phone on the empty pillow beside me. I pulled the duvet over my shivering body and rested my tear stained cheek on the matching pillow beneath. Facing my phone, I curled into the fetal position. Cradling what was left of my heart, fearful that any sudden movement would lure me into oblivion.

I stared at my phone through sorrowful eyes. One hour melted into two, then three, four and five. I stopped counting after that and started praying.

Praying in desperation for my phone to ring.

I waited all night for you to fix me. I waited all night for you to call and you never did.

Plus De Fleurs

The sink was overflowing with stained pots and pans. The floor was covered in a film of dust that traced my every move. The bathroom was rancid. The pungent smell of regurgitated food and vodka deterred me from eating.

My ribs start to protrude. I run my fingers across them like a xylophone as I replay the memories of the last two weeks. I close my eyes and I can smell the freshly baked cream puffs and dark roasted coffee he picked up from the family-owned coffee shop down the street. It was going to be a good day, a day like no other I surmised.

We sit around my wooden bistro breakfast table as he stretches his hand in front of him beckoning me to hold on. His hand is warm and sticky, proof of his impatience, as he must have had one of the cream puffs on his way home. I giggle at the thought; he sees the mirth in my eyes and knows that I've figured out his dirty little secret. Silently, we eat, in absolute reverence of each other.

I open my eyes and my palms are aching to brush against his. The fogged memory is whisked away by the wicked reality –he's not here. It's starting again, I can feel the moisture evaporate from my mouth as my empty stomach prepares itself for another bout of retching. I throw my head back in exasperation; angry at him, tired of missing him.

Just when I'm about to collapse into a fit of tears, the little energy I have left is channeled into sprinting to the bathroom. Before the pain escapes, I flip the lid of the toilet and fill it with my desolation. I decide to stay there for a minute with my hands wrapped around the ceramic bowl, cradling it, begging it with my embrace to feed me consolation.

Deliriously, I screw my eyes shut and start to traumatize myself with the memory of him. I can see his stiff body hanging from the reinforced pipe in the basement, his mouth agape gasping for the air he has deprived it of. Under his feet, wrapped in cheap brown floral tissue lays a bouquet of Casa Blanca lilies, but they are dying, chasing the fate of their purchaser.

I untie his body from its final noose; his skin is hard and waxy. The denial is deft, protecting me from the obvious. I whisper his name, not wanting to suddenly wake him.

"Baby, Justin, baby, Justin," I murmur as I press his cold cheek against my quivering lips. He doesn't respond –he can't respond.

Only when his body is being pulled away on the gurney do the tears come. They are hard pellets of relief that indignantly pour out of me. The sobs are stifling but without him, I am bound to suffocate, to wither away, to die with the sunrise, and bury myself with the moon.

"Come back, come back to me," I start to repeat as I pry my wet eyes open.

Relatable

"It will get better, don't worry, God will not
forsake you," they say in an attempt to soothe me.

I stare at them underneath weary lids wishing –
no praying, that if there is a God and if he does
care about me he stitches their mouths shut.

For I am too far-gone to put my pathetic life in the
hands of faith. I need more, like a hot bullet to the
brain to finally ease this ache.

The Next One

The next guy I dated only had to meet one criterion: he couldn't be sick like me. He had to be mentally stable enough for the love I had to give.

The next guy I dated was too stable for me, he couldn't understand the dimensions of my insanity.

The next guy I dated told me I was too sick, to seek help, to be a normal girl, only then could he ever commit to loving me.

One Night Stand

It was nothing more than a dalliance. A quick burn of desire covered in fleshy overalls. I learned then that our favor lies not with perpetuity but with the deep appreciation of knowing when to let a man go.

I don't know if it's the right thing to do but it is equally painful to want someone who has already forgotten you.

Unveiling

I hate being sober and facing this shit alone. The heartache goes off like an alarm in my head every hour or so.

And when it does, the emblem of pain manifests itself. I'm forced to wear it like the stench of a harlot after a long night of paid services.

The disappointment is rank; you could smell it through my denim. I set myself up for this, falling in love with boys who only care about peeling away my clothes.

Unaware that with each thrust my dilapidated heart is being exposed.

Extracurricular Heartbreak

I was a bystreet to you, a small lane with a scenic view. You walked the length of me until there was nowhere left to go.

That was when I learned that men break hearts for sport when they are bored.

The Truth

"Why are you sad?"

"Because I've fallen in love and I know it won't last."

"You sound certain."

"I am –he's only with me because it's convenient."

Commit To Change

I grew restless waiting for you to care. So I took
my heart back and settled on ending our affair.
Right when I garnered enough strength to walk
away, you stopped me to plead, "Don't give up
yet. I'm going to change."

I've wasted time waiting for that change to come.

You lied, but I believed you.

So who was really wrong?

Talented

Some sing, some dance, some paint, some play instruments.

My talent has always been *fucking* things up; overthinking the simplest notions and running amok.

Musician

He sang between my legs a song I will never
forget. The tune syrupy slow, the heat of his
breath chilled between my thighs. I danced to his
rhythm but he held me tight and told me to stop.

So I stilled my shallow breath and waited for the
chorus to come.

And when it came, I knew I would never be able
to get his stupid song out of my head again.

Underneath It All

"Do you think we'll ever get it right?" she said as she fell onto her back to appreciate the skies.

"I hope so," I shrugged as I mimicked her actions and relaxed onto my back. Blades of dewy grass pricked me through my cotton shirt, but I ignored it, sensing that such discomfort was worth the conversation we were about to have.

"Look at us, here, heartbroken and sad, forgetting the beauty in the vastness of the universe. It shouldn't matter this much, this stupid pain is infinitesimal, yet it's consuming me," she pauses as she waits for the right words to fall on her tongue, "it hurts so badly, everywhere, all of me, yet I don't know where to remedy."

Her honesty scared me but I understood what she meant. I propped myself up on my elbow to look at my friend only to realize the glistening wet streaks pouring from the corners of her eyes. I wondered if I should launch forward to pull her into my arms or pretend that I didn't notice. I settled for the latter, it's easier to peel back layers when people feel invisible.

"You'll get it right. We're young everything feels earth-shattering, we're so fucking sensitive right now," then I remembered that I too have gotten it wrong so many times so I correct myself, "we'll get it right."

As the silence stretched between us I felt the cogs in her brain turning, weaving together how she really felt.

"When you're sad, life feels like it's going too slow, relishing in your agony then when you're happy you wish it would just slow down. Allow you to prolong the *joie de vivre*. Life is either too long or too short for us. I suppose that's its signature punishing rhythm."

Raven

Her hair falls like loose autumn leaves all over her face as the burn initiated her haze.

"How many drinks have you had?"

"Not enough," she slurs.

She smudges her lipstick on then spits in her palms and pushes it through her greasy limp hair. She takes a moment to drink in her reflection from the tinted SUV window, surprisingly she likes what she sees, but then I remember she's barely seeing.

"Do I look good?" she asks as we enter the club.

"Yes you do," I lie.

They call her name and she stumbles onto the stage –the crowd loves seeing her like this. She rocks her hips as the bass guitarist strums the opening chords. A singular light shines right on her, everything else is cloaked in darkness.

I'm watching her from backstage as the forgetfulness ebbs and flows. One minute she's coherent and the next she's forgotten the next line to her song so she hums or steps away downplaying her alcohol-induced amnesia.

But no matter how drunk she got, her voice was always angelic, in stark contrast to her liquid demons. She belts out note after note that slams into my chest with chilling emotions. Finally, the performance is over.

"Did they like it?" her pleading tone, tugging for reassurance.

"They sure did," I reply truthfully.

We head to the car and she slides in the backseat. She reaches in her bag and takes a drink from her flask.

My swan is fleeting again, here comes the troubled raven. She starts to stumble over her own words. I'm tempted to grab the flask and throw it out the window, but I hesitate, not wanting to save her from her salvation.

"I hate this," she mumbles.

"Hate what?"

"This," she says as she shoves the flask in front of her, shakes it, then takes another sip.

"Then stop."

"Yeah," she replies before taking another drink drowning herself in alcohol to escape reality.

The Call To Salvation

I talked my friend out of suicide once. She was disoriented and drunk. It started that Monday when he called her to end things. On Sunday, my phone rang and she was on the other end. She had a single blade to her wrist, ready to open her veins and bleed agony.

"What the fuck are you doing? Please don't do this."

I started getting ready to go to her house, to stop my friend from leaving us. I kept her on the phone as a distraction, telling her things I didn't believe, praying to a God we weren't even sure existed. When I got to her apartment, she greeted me at the door. The faint red mark across her wrist where the blade autographed too obvious to ignore.

I looked at her and she stared back until I grabbed her in my arms and hugged her. I hugged her so tight for so long, pushing her broken pieces against mine. We fell to the floor in each other's embrace. I felt the sadness sinuously leak from her pores to escape. When I finally was brave enough to let her go, there were no words left to say.

We fell asleep cuddled together on the floor. My chest full of the appreciation that she wasn't gone.

119

I knew my friend was tethering on the edge, trying to hold on, but I tell her every day that if she didn't want me to save her, then she wouldn't have called.

Missed Call

My mother called me one day and I didn't
answer. I was only tired and I couldn't muster up
the courage to fake the type of happiness that
would put her at ease. She panicked. My mother
thought that I was dead. One missed call and she
thought I was no longer here. She's not
overprotective so don't think that. My mother
knew how sad I was, how broken I had become.

She knew suicide at that point was an option.

Love On Dark, Womanly Things

I am beaten and misused, a conundrum of melancholic emotions. I was crawling, pleading for second chances with people who saw my bloodied knees not with passion but with pity. The scars on my back are hardened and raised, they are ugly and in times like, this they feel brand new. The cut may not bleed but it is raw.

They pulled the light out of me and then wondered why I was so dark. They saw the tears behind fake smiles and pretended to be blind. On my brightest days, it still felt like I was living in a shadow of the life I deserved. Can you imagine the weight of a pain so solely carried?

They pushed me into crater deep pits and extended a short hand, yelling at me to rise from a pit that was designed to keep me there forever. The bruises, the chaos, the ongoing torture of being in a torpid state; I can never be happy.

I am an unfinished sonnet, a chapter rewritten with a dismal ending. This void has imbibed every drop of hope I had in me. Then when I rush to the bathroom at two in the morning and throw my head against the hollow walls they say I'm crazy. I'm not crazy, I'm a sad, lonely woman going through womanly things.

Overwhelmed

These four walls can't confine me, yet I am confined within them. Afraid that if I step outside the sunlight will illuminate what I've been trying to hide.

The sunken holes in my face where I used to have eyes. I have not rested. *How can I rest?* When I close my eyes all I see and feel is hell. The devil gleefully prepares my bed. So I stop sleeping, I stay awake and then I daydream about hell.

Four walls can't confine me, yet here I am hiding my sadness behind them.

Stranger In My Own Skin

I'm living in a home that doesn't belong to me, the blinds are open but I can't see. The walls are lopsided and the hallways are steep. I can't get out but the incubus gets in, he tends to my skin with a scourge made out of my diffidence and laughs through the wailing, underpinning my chagrin.

I'm living in a home that doesn't belong to me – it belongs to demons veiled as people and the adjectives they use to describe me.

I'm living in a home that does not belong to me, but how do I go elsewhere when this home is my skin?

Agenda

Option 1: A bullet to the brain
Option 2: Carbon monoxide
Option 3: Jumping off a building
*Option 4: Sleeping pills then place a plastic bag over
my head*
Option 5: Hanging

The last option seemed the easiest.

Monday: Too soon I need time to prepare
Tuesday: I promised my friend I'd go to the movies
Wednesday: Laundry
Thursday: Destroy my diary, tidy my room
Friday: Write note

Friday seemed like the best day because I hated
spending weekends alone.

Friday 8:00 a.m. - Today is the day
Friday 9:00 a.m. - Take a shower
Friday 10:00 a.m. - Call mother
Friday 11:00 a.m. – Get mother's longest scarf
Friday 12:00 p.m. - Do it

I looked at my phone and grabbed the scarf,
headed into the bathroom and worked out how I
would do it, the perfect height, the perfect drop. I
tied one end on the inside knob, threw the scarf
over the door, closed the door, wrapped the other

end around my neck, time to let my body do the rest.

I say a quick prayer, asking for forgiveness, then I hear my phone ring, it's my mother –she's calling me to open the gate.

Her phone call stalled my plans.

Help Me Please

"I'm sick."

"The flu, a headache, food poisoning?"

"No, but I would trade anything to be ill in body."

Therapy Session

"Every motion and thought is reduced to the unfortunate rhythm of routine and sadness," is what I said to my therapist when she asked me to describe my life.

She stopped taking notes to give me some consoling eye contact. It took her a while to descry my vulnerability and when she did I saw the guilt. Even in the throes of her guilt, I knew it'd be hard for her to save me.

 I was emotionally void. Sitting in her plush red chair was the ghost of the girl she thought she was talking to. My eyes were heavy and tired. I had grey hairs sprouting from the base of my hairline and crow's feet that found permanent residence at the corners of my eye. The unfamiliar weariness was finally the norm for me.

 I told her that I stopped taking the sleeping pills but it was a lie. Each night I placed two, three, or four on my tongue, then cuffed my hands to gather the water from the faucet to help the pills along.

What happened to me? What was the root of my pain? It was him, it was her, it was school, it was work, it was my mother, it was my father. It was the world.

133

I'd lost myself trying to please everyone and when I broke down no one knew.

When I reached out for help, they told me to *cheer up,* as if flowery words were the solution, miraculous enough to help me pull through.

It Was Always There

You can only pretend to not be broken for so long,
and when you can't pretend anymore they have
the audacity to ask, *"Where did this all sadness come
from?"*

Temptation

I am tempted to end it all again, to finally be
sheathed in dirt. Lowered six feet beneath this
ghastly world so I can feed the hungry vermin
and nourish the soil.

Who would miss me?

Here, right now, no one sees me; yet, here right
now, I am suffering.

I Will Never Forget What You Did

With a mouthful of blood, all she could do was stare. Her eyes pleading for my silence. He raised his hand then brought it down with a burning vengeance that seared her already bruised flesh.

His hands bloodied and swollen, he grimaced with pain each time it made hard contact with her raw skin. The wall behind her was stained with the history of his abuse. I peer through the balusters; horrified and confused when she finally goes silent.

I think he is done when he pulls his foot back, like a finger pulling the elastic of a slingshot. He gathers some momentum before he thrusts it into her lower abdomen. Her body reacts violently by spitting blood onto his steel toe boots. Contented, he turns around and heads to the kitchen to ice his swollen knuckles. When the coast is clear, I crawl down the stairs and over to her. Her shirt looks like abstract art, lots of red in all sizes scattered across the front.

I take the end of my sleeve and wipe away some of the blood from the corner of her lips, she moans drearily. I try to make her look okay again; pushing away some of her hair but it's stuck to her forehead, plastered there by her blood and sweat, testament to all she's endured.

Her placid brown eyes now eclipsed with clots. I kneel there in front of her for as long as possible, not wanting to leave her defenseless again. I bite my tongue, refusing to say anything that could wound her any further.

Suddenly, her swollen eyes start to widen as she stares behind me, the panic leaves her eyes and goes straight into mine, before I can register what is about to happen I feel his cold hands lift me to my feet.

He spins me around and drops his gaze to meet mine. The towel he has wrapped around his fist is drenched in blood. He sees that I'm piecing together what has happened so he bends down and kisses me on my forehead, his kindness confusing, shrouded with insincerity.

 I smile shyly at him, hiding the torrent of emotions within me. I want to scream, kick and fight him but his *go to your room honey*, sends my white flag of surrender up into the air. As much as I want to put some distance between us, I'm afraid to leave her alone with him again. He senses my hesitation.

"What's wrong honey?" he says in an all too sweet tone.

"Can she come with me?"

"No honey, she's not feeling well, but don't worry I'll take care of her like I always take care of you," he says.

His chilling words, force a stray tear from my eye and I beg the heavens that he won't touch her again, at least not for the rest of the night.

Inheritance

If bruised skin and split lips are all you see. You'll
wake up one day, twenty-three, asking yourself,
when did the battered lover, become me?

The Last Straw

He was drinking that night.

Violently, he pulled the sheets from the bed and I tried to tell him to be quiet. He was so loud, telling me that tonight he was going to, *fuck my brains out*. I never saw this side of him before. He yanked me to the edge of the bed, forcing my oversized t-shirt to ride all the way up to my stomach. At first, I jokingly protested, gently swatting him away, not wanting to add fuel to his burning fire. His eyes became dark, poisoned with an ungovernable sexual appetite that terrified me.

"You know you want this," he mumbled.

He was looking right at me but he couldn't see me. My playful protest was replaced with the fight or flight rush of adrenaline. I pushed him away and ran into the bathroom. I pressed my back against the door, frightened of the man I loved, the man who I wanted to spend the rest of my life with.

The panic rose like a rocket in my chest. I remember him banging against the door yelling " open the door bitch!" and " I'll give you something to cry about!" With each brute word, my fear delved deeper and deeper into my body anchoring itself in my heart and forcing me to cry.

"Please you're drunk, stop this," I said in between sobs.

There came a point when I could not tell the difference between him banging on the door and my heart pounding in my chest. The loud bangs sent vibrations through my jellified limbs. I closed my eyes pleading for him to stop, even to my own ears I sounded unfamiliarly desperate. After a few minutes, everything went eerily silent. From thunderous bangs to dead silence, my ears quickly adapted to the change.

My senses were no longer overwhelmed, everything became sharp again, so I pressed my right ear against the door carefully listening to the other side. There was nothing to be heard but the rush of blood moving from my brain to my body. I thought to myself that maybe he fell asleep. Maybe the alcohol took him into a slumber. Slowly, I opened the door, the slow creak of its hinges almost unnerving to hear. My legs forgot how to walk, so intently, I placed one foot in front of the other, stepping out of my fortress. Two steps later and there he was sitting on the bed staring at me.

The blood in the soles of my feet curdled, sending a shockwave of paralytic fear straight up my body. My eyes had widened so much I was sure that they were going to fall out of my head at any second. He looked up but never fully lifted his head, instead his head started to slowly dance side-to-side like a snake charmer seducing the venomous creature. He licked his lips and a sinister grin snuck across his face. He tilted his head to the left measuring my fear and enjoying the chilling mood between us. He looked down and onto his hands and for a brief second I thought all would be well.

Then he stood up slowly and intently, he wasn't bobbing and swaying like a drunkard. His precise militant march towards me sent my breathing into a frenzy. My chest rose and fell like an asthmatic about to have an attack. I should have run, I know I should have, but my feet never moved. By the time he stood in front of me, his stature eclipsed my body.

"I am a going to fuck you and there is nothing you can do about it," were the only words he thought I deserved to hear.

My body was smarting from his bitter words. I watched on as he leaned down and started to kiss me, the scent of his drunkenness almost nauseating. He wrapped my ponytail around his hand and tugged hard, leaving my neck exposed to the vile movements of his wet tongue. My body's slavish response to my fears betrayed my urge to run, giving him the full advantage. He moaned as his hands explored my body, and finally, when he had enough of his foreplay, he pushed me onto the bed. The spike in my blood pressure compelled me to fight back, but my strength was diminished so I begged again for him not to do this. I begged and I begged in vain.

In one swift motion, he was on top of me. His punishing rhythm should have hurt but the numbness protected me. I turned my head to the side as he assaulted my body, I stared at a picture on the wall of us as kids. The younger me in the picture wept inconsolably as my body jerked back and forth. I lost my soul as he gained an orgasm and lulled himself to sleep. His euphoria came at the expense of my dignity.

It was the culmination of all my mistakes, being ravaged by a man I thought I loved forced my demons out. It was time to face them, sit them down, it was time to leave my old life. The life where everyone took advantage of me was finally done.

The Philosophy Of Mind & Body

They run their filthy hands all over your pure
skin and expect you to know the difference
between loving and lusting. They call you *baby*,
babe, and *honey* as if you were their girlfriend then
laugh you to scorn when you express your
feelings.

Their minds and bodies are separate entities so
they assume ours must be wired with the same
duality. But when you touch my body in the right
ways, my mind ignites, it starts to blaze. It burns
like a lantern that pierces through the blanket of
darkness and blooms between my legs like the
Casa Blanca lily at nights.

So, if you touch my body, graze it with even the
most impure hands, you've touched other parts of
me, you've stained my mind.

The Beloved

Rehab

I am not some hollow basin for you to fill with your desires. I'm not that little girl whose veins crave your poison anymore. I have no interest in your lines either, those tidy white lines of lies you forced underneath my nose. You are unimportant and pernicious to all that I can become.

You are a crippling drug, the worst addiction that I've ever overcome.

Bloody Words

I had a man raise his hand to my face, so hard was the impact that when I opened my mouth the blood trickled out. He looked remorseful and scared; I was still in shock. He stepped forward to hold me in an apologetic gesture, one that the girl I was would've accepted.

But I stepped back from him and his tempered hands. With stained teeth and a sore mouth, I spat in his face, the deep red saliva conveying my anger. Before his hand delivered its brutality again, I grabbed it mid-air and pushed it away.

"Don't you ever put your fucking hands on me again!"

Realization

I crept over our tangled clothes and tiptoed into the bathroom where the fluorescent lights embellished my sin. I tried to wash it away with a scalding shower. I scrubbed so hard my skin felt raw after. I wrapped myself in the fluffy white towel and wiped the fogged mirror to get a better view of the whore in the reflection.

Two hours later, he asked me what was wrong. He was curious as to why I was so silent at lunch. I shrugged and told him today just wasn't my day.

I'm a monster. I cheated on you, was what I really wanted to say.

I never thought I could hurt someone but I was carrying scars that turned me into a cancerous person. I started to act like those who I condemned. I hated them so much that I slowly became them.

Blame

I never took responsibility for any of my actions. I always blamed the men for it was easier to play the victim than it was to face the demented little girl in my head.

Eponymous

Say their name,
The person who broke you, the person who
comes to mind when you kiss the one you've
settled for
Say their name,
The one whose scent still lingers on your bed and
seeps through your pores
Say their name,
The one who vacated your life but has never left
your thoughts
Say their name,
The one who stained your skin with marks of love
 Say their name,
The one who held your neck and slammed you
against the wall, stuck a tongue down your throat
and pulled lust out of you like an animal
Say their name,
The one who carried you to the edge of sanity and
fucked you back to the calm
Tell me their name, so I can hold your hand and
stitch you together with understanding
Tell me their name, so I can preach the
unbelievable story about how it'll get better in
time
Please, tell me their name so you won't go home,
shove your head into the pillow and scream it
tonight

Spiritus

The breaths we take after a breakup start off
ragged and forced. Timid inhalations of crisp air
because we don't want our lungs to touch our
sore hearts.

A shallow breath is how I survived my breakup,
no words of wisdom, no rebound, no life-
affirming novels. I allowed my heart to revel in its
damage, soaking up all the pain at its disposal.

I thought if I allowed my heart to sap away my
sadness there would be none left. Like a dirty old
washcloth, I used my heart to clean it all away,
the memories, the lies, the hope of reconciliation,
everything. My heart begged to be relinquished
from such an arduous task but I took small
shallow breaths and told it *no*.

It was the only way to move on, breathing fresh
air through these old tired lungs.

Shell Of Myself

When he left he took everything with him. My dignity, my sanity, and strength followed him through the door. The only thing he left behind was a gaping wound in my chest where my heart used to be and my corpse.

So I thought I couldn't exist without a man's love.

Then the impossible happened and I started to exist all on my own.

Easy

I stopped envying those who led easy lives, for they underestimate the power of the weak and those crippled by adversities.

They have no idea what it's like to walk through life with broken feet.

Mommy

The first time I spoke darkness to her, she cried, terrified that such menacing words had found a home in my vocabulary.

"*Oh*, ma, please don't cry –this is why I didn't want to tell you."

"I always knew you were keeping secrets but this –if you ever –it would've been the end of me."

I understood the consternation in her voice but hoped she understood the anguish in mine. If she didn't then I'd know I could never confide in her again and what good is a mother if she can't be your best friend?

"I am sorry," she uttered between sobs.

"For what?"

"For making you ever doubt I would understand."

Honest Interactions

"When did you realize you wanted to live?"
asked my mother.

"That's not the realization that saved my life –not
hiding anymore, not pretending I was fine is what
changed things for me. I started wanting to live
when I shamelessly accepted that I was sick."

Be Yourself

Be yourself, was what everyone continued to tell me. It was a popularized fallacy that somehow being *you* would solve everything. Life would get exponentially better if you gave into your identity; clearly, the people who continue to spread this lie have never met someone like me.

Innately, I am a terrible person, not to those around me but to myself. I am the victim of my own darkness. I am evil to my core, rotten to my soul, and I have no great ambitions. So the best version of myself would be me, stiff as a board in a coffin.

I can't be myself.

Instead, I'm pulling the best attributes from those around me –I don't want to be them. But unlike me, they have redeeming qualities that I can piece together and be decent. I'm smart enough to discern the good in people but too foolish to see any of those qualities within me.

Be yourself applies to the beautifully sane, not me.

California Dreaming

The record-breaking heat made my sweat slicken skin feel like it was baking. My apartment was too small and tight for even one person, but it was all I could afford. No A/C, no modern appliances, just one lonely girl, four walls, and dirty sheets.

Alone and overheating I started to think, *will my life ever get any better than this?*

I suppose it will.

The Narcissist

What actual shame is there in being a narcissist?
To be someone who wraps their skin in praise,
whose rapacious self-love offends all others
because of its intensity?

What actual shame is there in being a narcissist?
To see people through windows of utility, well, if
that's so wrong then don't we all have narcissistic
tendencies?

What actual shame is there in being a narcissist?
Exaggerating your importance, bolstering your
confidence, articulating your worth with actions
and language –sounds like heaven to me.

What actual shame is there in being a narcissist?
Please, someone, explain, because I only know
what it is like to tear through my hideous skin. To
shun my reflection and exercise extreme levels of
self-hatred.

One Wonderful Night

We danced skin to skin, our bodies moved in unison. It was a night blurred with insipid liquor and instinctual attraction. His hands snaked over my skin to find its resting place on the nape of my neck. He led my face to his and under the strobe lights and pulsating music we kissed. He tasted like a bad decision and vodka, but I was too swept away in the moment, my consciousness barely able to absorb everything around me.

When the music died down and the once-crowded dance floor emptied, he grabbed my hand and said *come with me.* We spilled into the streets clumsily; excitement and fatigue stole our elegance. We were shrouded in darkness for most of the night so it took a minute for our eyes to adjust to the harsh streetlights. I paused for a moment to slip out of my heels, and then I looked back at him, his handsome tired face beaming.

I laughed as we skipped down the street gyrating to the music between the palm trees. Suddenly, I remembered my hunger, I looked over to him with a sheepish grin and he said, "I want to eat, let's get pizza. You must be starving."

He told me jokes and stroked the back of my shoulder as we ate our pizza and guzzled down our beer. After satisfying our hunger, we sauntered into the empty streets once again. I kept turning around to kiss him, and each time it got harder to stop, my appetite insatiable, I couldn't resist him. Our energetic tryst started to wind down, so we sat on the curb and gave each other that look.

As the sun rose from its slumber, it dawned on me that I had spent an entire night with someone who made me genuinely happy. As the dark skies bled hues of orange and pink, he looked to me once again and said that tonight, undoubtedly has been one of the best nights of his life, but he was afraid another night together wouldn't be this nice.

I agreed. So I scheduled an Uber to come and get me, in the five minutes between confirming my ride and its arrival we kissed. We kissed and kissed until the wheels of an unfamiliar car slowed in front of us. It was my driver waiting for me to get in. I wanted to tell him to come with me. But there's something innately beautiful about something so amazing like this being short-lived.

He gave me one last kiss and I thanked him for everything. I had fun, a sad girl like me found excitement in spontaneity. So thank you amazing stranger for my one night of bliss.

It Ends Before We End It

The worst part of a breakup isn't the ending at all. It's the days before when something seems off. When you start to slowly feel things fall apart. So you scrape together thinly veiled lies to tell yourself, like how it is a phase or a rough patch because you forgot that it could end. As the heart braces itself for the beating it's about take, it puts your insecurities on display.

So you try harder. Forcing yourself to do things you would have never done before, like anxiously overthinking anything they do that's unusual.

We're dutiful to our relationships when we know their ending. Straining our hearts to continue what is already fading.

Full Cup

Like the sun pouring through the blinds as it
rises, the truth from my drunken mouth awoke
us.

"You hate me?"

"With every inch of me," I whispered in shame.

"Why –how –you're too drunk right now."

"But my thoughts are sober. I am speaking the
truth. You ridicule my feelings, you unthread my
self-esteem, you cheat, you lie, and you expect
because I'm some dull-witted gal for me to ignore
all of this –I did –not anymore. I hate you."

Double Edged Sword

My flaw has always been that I feel everything deeply; my strength will always be that I feel everything deeply.

Lana

Our souls escape from their silos as Lana echoes through the small hall. My shoulders roll back and forth, his waist slowly moves side to side as her voice slips beneath our wet clothes, unbuckling him, unbuttoning me.

"Touch me."

"Where?"

"Everywhere," I reply slowly and bite down on my lower lip. His eyes widen and his jaw slackens as he finally catches on. His carnal smile is my undoing –the perfect response to send my body crashing into his.

Where he ends, I begin. Him, Lana and I invite a night full of passionate lovemaking.

Faux Savage

I tried to be a savage once, the girl who buries her
delicacy underneath a hard and coarse
exoskeleton.

I tried to be a savage once but it hurt more than
being soft. I had to force callousness out of my
mouth then pretend to be unaffected by it all.

I tried to be a savage once and kick men down,
like that was the answer, like it was helpful,
breaking hearts, mocking feelings, taking them
for granted.

I tried to be a savage once until I realized I broke
someone's heart, and they would go on
distrusting women because of me and how I tore
them apart.

I tried to be a savage once and I had to stop, it
didn't make sense to be heartless in a world that
needed love.

Things I Wish Someone Would Say To Me

I love you.

Not with my heart but with my entire being, the constellation of stars, the moon, and the sun. This love cannot roam free *–oh* what chaos it would cause if this love was free.

My love, this love is cataclysmic –a powerful yet understated storm that brews on the brim of exciting.

Poets have written it, artists have painted it, and musicians have played it, yet here I am speaking it.

I love you.

Every inch of your skin, those pores, every strand of your hair, I cannot be satisfied. My appetite too large to ever grow tired of any morsel you choose to feed me. I'll take the scraps as long as you help me to free this love, unchain it from my lungs so I can finally breathe.

 I love you, foolishly, wholeheartedly, and without exhaustion.

So please, love me.

Unread

The text was still flashing across the screen, tirelessly trying to seduce me. I grabbed my phone and almost gave in, but then I remembered all the times that I texted him. The lengthy paragraphs that I drafted five or six times before sending, only to be underwhelmed and frayed by his monosyllabic responses.

I started to shake, anxious and indecisive, torn between our history and new beginnings. *Maybe this time things would be different, maybe this time he would be more cognizant of what he did.* Who was I trying to fool?

If I answered his text I would be bound and gagged with abuse. And on this new journey my heart was set on fulfilling, a man like him needed to be cut loose.

The First Lesson

I was never whole. I inherited my fault lines from my mother, the inescapable disadvantage of being her daughter. We were jars of broken pieces, rattling through life, destined to be doormats for those who took advantage of our insecurities.

I was never whole.

I am a puzzle of the woman I should be, so excuse me while I piece myself together then teach my mother everything she couldn't teach me.

Born Into It

When you're young your parents lie to you to build character. They tell you that you're special, you're beautiful, you can get anything you want. My father was unlike this, he reminded every day that I was nobody, that *special* was a word used to describe the inadequate, the ones without gifts.

He planted a seed that he watered with doubt, so I worked twice as hard, twice as long, –I worked hard to prove strangers wrong. Academically, this helped me to succeed but in the nights, the weight of his words bludgeoned my self-esteem.

I know he wanted great things for me, but when I was twelve and struggling with my identity, it was easy to believe that my protector, my father, didn't love me.

Light

I've wasted the best years of my life living angrily and in doubt. Now I'm hungry to live the rest of my life peacefully, above the old pain, floating in the clouds.

My Father's Repentance

Broken little girls hate their fathers for reasons unbeknownst to them. So they search for their fathers in unworthy men. I was one of them. Until I took the pieces of my broken heart and marched to my father's doorstep. I placed each piece in front of him and said, "You were the first man to break my heart, please help me fix it."

He was stunned by my honesty but respected my strength. He admitted where he went wrong and told me how much he wanted to repent. His hair was grey and his eyes spilled regret.

He put the last piece of my heart back together and with one whole healed heart, my quest for love felt completely different.

Mrs. N. Grant

Her hands were coarse and wrinkled. In the islands, grandmothers worked until their hands grew stiff. There was no luxurious retirement just unrelenting hard work. My grandmother was like yours. She had a broad back that carried the stresses of sons, daughters, grandkids, her husband, and even strangers. Her back never grew weak even after arthritis stole so much of her body.

My grandmother redefined womanhood for me. Her womanhood was not in her hips nor was it on her skin. Her womanhood came from the heat she felt on Sunday evenings cooking over a full stove. Her womanhood came from the bruised knees she got from cleaning floors. Her womanhood came from the sun peppering her skin while she pinned hand washed laundry to her crowded clothesline. Being a woman meant exercising her utility so when her usefulness started to wither so did she. Growing unable to do these things made her covet her sprier days, it stole something from her, something deep.

My grandmother was a teacher. Some lessons were so important she had to teach me twice. Like how the world would try to inject hate into my veins, but I must fight the urge to become like them because hate is not in my nature. It was a balance she hinted, being a woman and living through womanhood was an intricate balance. We must give but never give too much, we must use our voices, but never speak hatefully, and we must learn to brave the storm but never let it change us for the worse.

On Saturdays, we would pick peas from the pods as she hummed songs in off tones. I never recognized any of them but I knew all of them. Every Sunday she sat by the same window and stared outside as the cars raced by. I always felt the sadness of her gaze, as if she was wishing for something she could never regain. Her musing was magnetic but I feared one day she wouldn't return, she'd forget the present looking so deeply into the past.

So I'd tug on her sleeve and a warm smile would greet me as she reached into her purse for a piece of candy to give me. The candy was her way of saying, "I'm okay." Even as a young girl she saw the worry in my brows and the concern on my creaseless face. When she handed me the sweet we'd both stare at her hands as a tremor stole their steadiness. She'd quickly fold them into her lap and I'd pretend I didn't notice, but from the corner of my eye, I saw how she looked down on her hands, disappointed in their rapid deterioration.

After church, she'd gossip with her friends by my grandfather's car. They'd laugh and pat each other on the shoulder as they told stories and complimented outfits. In those moments, I'd get glimpses of who she was. A dainty young woman who rebelled gently, she who could tame a thousand fires with a whisper.

A young woman's life that could have been far more eventful, yet she chose to make it simple. She chose to live selflessly. We all do acts of kindness but she lived that way, opening her arms and extending her embrace to anyone willing to accept it. They didn't have to be in need or desperate when she touched their lives and scrubbed away their worries.

She did what she told me not to do, she gave too much and the world took without any remorse. She made me see just how much the world takes from women. The good women, the bad women, even the weak ones, the world's greed was non-discriminatory. Women like my grandmother fell victim to an appetite they could never satisfy and I think she knew that but she never stopped giving.

In the end, the breadth of her back is hardly remembered by anyone else. Those who ate from her scoured pots and scuffed the floors she bloodied her knees cleaning describe her as *nice*. A life of sincere greatness reduced to an overused adjective with little impactful meaning. I suppose when my skin goes cold and the rigor mortis sets in someone will do the same to me.

A life so brightly lived reduced to a frivolous term such as nice and a *shittily* worded obituary.

Incentive

I am healing. I am learning to pull splinters of sadness from my soul. I am crawling towards everything I thought I could never have: happiness, love, and sanity. I am falling apart, rebuilding myself with alabaster and patience. I am within and without, learning to appreciate the view of who I am to others and who I am to myself.

You are a part of this journey, you started it the moment you told me I was nothing.

Magic

I strained my neck, constantly looking up to those
who looked down on me. The sorcery of a broken
self-esteem, for I was lifting my head to those
who in reality were on the same level as me.

Discriminatory

If every hateful word you spat was painted across
my skin, I'd be a canvas full of your scripture, an
example of the virulence you preach. Only then
would someone like you see how acidulous a
tongue like yours could be.

The Anatomy of Forgetting

The heart's amnesia is a wickedly beautiful thing. For no matter how many times I've felt the blunt force of heartbreak tear through me, I somehow forget the pain and rediscover the strength to love again.

I suppose healing means renewed naivety, covering wounds like they never existed. It's one of the greatest attributes of mankind, loving, giving ourselves to someone else even when we know the risk of losing.

The Forgetful Side of Forgiveness

Let me forgive you, not for what you did but for who you almost turned me into. It took time and space for me to shed the shame you wrapped around my soul. To become, not the result of your mistreatment, but a by-product of my own.

I've forgiven you, for no other reason than I needed to forgive myself. You were churlish to me but I was the one who let you in. Forgiving you does not mean we'll be close again.

My type of forgiveness means understanding the misfortunes of my past but never reliving them.

They Were Wrong

I wonder if the people who left us behind because we were struggling ever miss us. You know the friends, family members, and lovers who belittled us and always had an issue.

Then again, should we care what they think? They left because they thought we wouldn't become anything. So, now that we're succeeding, I wonder if they reflect upon their decision with remorse or are they seething? Upset that we had unending potential embedded in us but they weren't patient or kind enough to help reveal it.

They were wrong about us, weren't they? There is strength in you and a fight in me that grows unaffected by anything the myopic might say. They were so damn convinced that we would fail. Now, look at how divine we are, tenacious and wise. We're soldiers fighting for ourselves with our eyes on the prize.

Garden of Eager Seeds

I was born into a society where impressing
strangers was paramount to even impressing
myself. I was told how others saw me was a direct
and irrefutable reflection of who I was. I was
taught that womanhood came with the
subversion of my identity. "I mattered but not as
much", "I was a woman but only when…" were
phrases stitched into the fabric of my existence.

I am unraveling those ideals and I am outgrowing
that society.

I hope you outgrow it with me.

Solid

"I don't love you anymore," he said.

He stood waiting for my world to slam against his bitter wall of words and shatter as if it were made of hand-blown glass.

He couldn't understand why I wasn't begging him to love me, or why I hadn't crashed to my knees and cradled his feet.

The woebegone, pathetic bitch matured; I wasn't deficient anymore, so him not loving me wouldn't be my undoing like before.

You're Perfect

I can't be perfect –I don't want to be. I like the scars on my wrists and I like drinking tequila in the morning.

I can't be perfect, how could I be? Three months ago, I swallowed a bottle full of pills because I thought I was ugly.

I can't be perfect, why? Because perfect is a maddening journey that I've yet to see anyone complete.

Circumstantial Selfishness.

I've never met anyone who was selfish when those around them reaped the benefits, did none of the suffering or the hard work, but got to relax and play.

I've only ever heard someone was selfish when those around them had nothing to suck away.

You Deserve More

I accepted their crumbs, convincing myself that a
small piece of something was better than nothing.
But as my appetite grew the morsels they threw
my way could no longer satisfy me. So I asked for
more and they laughed in my face. I accepted
their scraps for so long they thought it was what I
deserved.

With hot tears burning my eyes I had to walk
away. The irony, in trying to avoid having
nothing, I ended up with nothing anyway.

Save Some For You

Giving too much of yourself to the wrong person will leave you bankrupt. Not in hard currency, but it will drain you of your energy, happiness, and time. Giving too much of yourself to the wrong person is a bad habit that we trick ourselves into pretending we don't mind.

We thoughtlessly overextend ourselves for them, hopeful that one day they will reciprocate. They won't, you've spoiled them, so all they do now is unabashedly take.

Giving too much of yourself to the wrong person is an unforgivable sin. Not to God or any religious deity, but to yourself. Starving your soul to feed someone who can't care doesn't make you selfless, it makes you vulnerable and puts you on the highway to regret and self-pity. Giving too much of yourself to the wrong person is how wise girls like you end up looking like fools.

So give too much to no one and always save some of yourself for you.

Forget Me Not

Like the cast of a hand left in wet cement; like the stain of a glass of wine that carelessly fell on your white carpet.

Like the impression of a tooth that bit too hard into fleshy lips; like the scars from the surgery you underwent.

Like the wounds of a soldier who fought wars that didn't belong to him.

Like the unforgiving burn of our sun on the first summer morning.

Forget me never, not today nor tomorrow, not even through the unrelenting sorrow.

Embers of Failures

I started to think that I was the problem. That who I was diametrically opposed what I wanted from life. I felt like a speck in the abyss of my own existence. My ambitions too large to fit into my miniature hands.

I wept when I thought there was no way I could ever become the woman I wrote about in my diaries. She, who embodied fire, blazed paths and burned through adversities with warmth and optimism.

I fell so low and laid so flat against the cold base of my heart that I could hear the murmurs of my broken dreams. Annoyed and frustrated with the constant whispers of my failures, I used those murmurs as tinder and started a small fire in my heart.

For most of my life, I searched for a way to start a fire within myself. Covered in the mess of who I was and haunted by the bruises of defeat, I started that fire and it hasn't stopped burning since.

Returning the Unfavorable Favor

You asked for the light and I reached into the night sky and gave you the stars. You asked for an answer and I gave you a bible full of truths. You turned to me with hungry eyes and I overfed you. You asked for honesty and I abandoned my reticence. You asked for a hand and I gave you every limb. You said you were tired of running so I walked with you. You begged for calm so I whispered when there were raging fires within. You asked for beauty so I splashed paint across our blank canvas. You wanted words so I gave you paragraphs.

I asked you for light and you gave me a shadow. I asked for an answer and you gave me your serpentine tongue. I turned to you with hungry eyes and you fed me crumbs. I asked for honesty and you gave me your taciturn countenance. I asked for a hand and you only moved a finger. I said I was tired of running so you ran without me. I begged for calm but all you gave me were raging fires. I asked for beauty and you painted my world grey. I wanted words so you gave me empty pages.

So now when you ask me for the light, and I give you the shade, I hope you understand. Next time before you look to me with hungry eyes, devour your own flesh. If you want honesty I will deafen you with silence. That hand that you want from me is busy, wrapped around myself. When you can't keep up with the pace of the world, I will not stop living my life to help. If you want the calm, I suggest a long slumber akin to death. When you ask for beauty, I will show you monsters. Those long paragraphs are now blank pages and unanswered texts.

We are even now, for I will give to the world what I get. No parasite like you shall take me for granted again.

A Text *(February 14, 2018)*

"Where can I go to find that type of love? Strong enough to withstand the riptides of life yet malleable enough to change with me. Firm enough to cocoon me in comfort but lax enough to give me room to grow. Where can I go to find that type of love?"

"First within you, then within them," she said.

Persona Non Grata

I wrote to her one last time. We'd grown apart,
trying to be a part of each other's life, but I knew.
I knew that who I became threatened her. She was
terribly afraid of me and all that I was capable of.
She couldn't cheer me on, the fear had stolen her
spirit.

As much as I loved her and wanted her to stay,
my life changed and with that change, she lost her
space. The distance too wide to ever bridge with
words. I knew this was the last time I'd write to
her.

She was old skin, too porous to hold me in. She
was bitter, too callous to understand and forgive.
She was weak, too feeble to defend me. I penned
those thoughts to her with necessary respites,
fatigued by the pain this would bring.

The skies parted and wept for us, letting the old
me go was the worst best thing that I could have
ever done.

The Teacup

Some days I want to inhale crisp air through someone else's lungs. See the beauty and monstrosity of man through a foreigner's eyes. Touch things I'm afraid of with the hands of someone fearless. Say words and phrases with a language that is not mine.

Some days I yearn to be anyone but me, anywhere but here and anything but this.

On those days, I see no adventure in my life, no triumph in my struggle, a scorned reflection, and wasteful existence. A dark vacant soul inhabits my being. A green-eyed beast peers through the cracks sipping the last drop of happiness from its champagne flute. I am left arid and famished for the one thing I cannot have, the one person I cannot be, and the one place I cannot go.

Some days, stuck with reality, I place my teacup on my windowsill. Through this window, the hues of orange and pink lift the blinds of my soul, awash with life's beauty, transfixed by its grace. Here, I do not want to see the world through someone else's eyes, my view will do.

Here, I no longer want to breathe through another's lungs, I can exhale through my own. Now, I have no need to touch things that make me cower with a distant hand, my hands are emboldened. Now, I can speak my language, exhibit my mastery.

On these days, I am enough, basking in the lightness of my once heavy shoulders. Appreciative of the scars from battles I am still fighting. On these days, the corners of my lips slowly tug apart, content with all my flaws.

Waltzing With The Sea

The cool white sand presses between my toes. My feet sink into the grains as I yank them out, doubling my effort to get where I need. Where the waves caress the shoreline the sand is dense and hard, yet the ocean pulls it away with enviable ease –I hope it does the same to me.

My sprint turns into a struggled jog as the water starts to rush against me. First, my ankles are submerged, then my knees. It's cold and I feel like a conscious drunk as I try to maintain my balance against the sea.

My satin silk wrap dress starts to feel heavy as the waves turn and twist at my waist, but I fight back, fastidious in my insanity. My arms stop swinging back and forth, as the icy water swallows them underneath so I start scooping away the sea, shoveling water, pulling myself deeper and deeper into her.

Suddenly, it's touching my shoulders and I know it's only a matter of time before I'm completely beneath, so I start calming myself, counting breaths, readying my exhausted body.

It happens quickly, I hear the world around me become muffled until it's finally silent. In the absence of everything worldly, my body starts to

243

listen to me. I'm suspended beneath the ocean as the floor falls away from me. My eyes are screwed shut, as I start to float I feel the weight of my sadness leave me. My dress dances around my hips, my hair stretches above, longing for the gravity of the surface. Seconds turn into minutes as I start to slowly feel it coming –the rationality.

Stay away, I think to myself as I feel my instincts creeping in, but I'm losing, my body betrays me. My eyes shoot open as my chest tightens, the calmness I hear is replaced by a ringing in my ear. I am thirsty for a breath but I want to stay here. Involuntarily, my mouth opens and it takes immense power to not take a deep breath. I tamp my hands over my mouth and start kicking. My throat starts to burn, my nose blows large bubbles as I try not to inhale –I'm scared.

I continue kicking until I can see the moonlight dancing on the face of the sea, I rush to her, I rush to the light –the light that will save me. I break the surface and my mouth falls open, everything comes crashing back into me. The air, the noise, the smell of the world, my lungs expand and for the first time in many years, I start to breathe.

Before I Go, Remember This

You are undoubtedly the sunrise and sunset of your own life.

They are the hours in between, not the sun that awakes you or the moon that puts you to sleep.

The End

Thank you Benjamin for the beautiful cover art and inspiration. I am forever indebted to you my love.

And to my family and friends, my journey would've ended far too early without your love and support.

Thank you for giving me hope.

I love you.

Made in the USA
Columbia, SC
12 October 2018